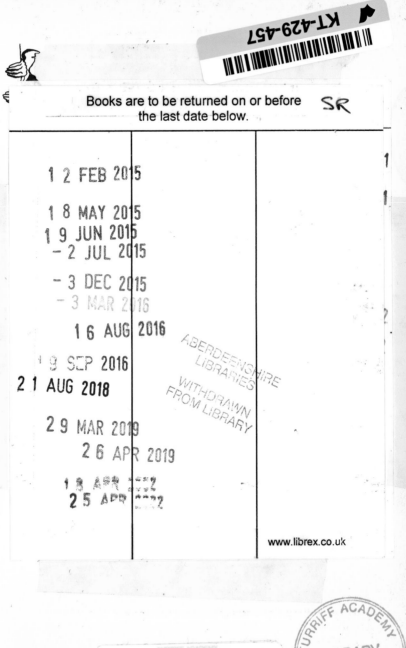

KT-429-457

First published in 2007 in Great Britain by
Barrington Stoke Ltd
18 Walker Street, Edinburgh EH3 7LP

www.barringtonstoke.co.uk

ISBN: 978-1-84299-463-4

Printed in Great Britain by Bell & Bain Ltd

A Note from the Author

I read in the paper about gangs of kids who set things on fire, then throw stones at the fire-fighters when they come to tackle the blaze. That got me thinking – why would anyone want to do something like that? I thought, maybe they're the sort of kids no one ever notices. You know – the middle kid in a family of three. The kid with a clever brother and sister. The kid whose mum and dad don't give a stuff anyway. If you were one of those kids, you'd feel like you didn't matter. As if you weren't really there at all.

Nothing big's ever going to happen because of *you*.

But what about a fire? A fire's big, and all you need is a match. Start a fire and you've made something happen. Something big. Flames in the sky, blue lights flashing and sirens wailing, pictures on the news. All because of you. Now you matter. Now they're taking notice.

Of course, I could be wrong about the reason. But there are reasons why people do stuff like that. This is Josh Linfoot's.

Contents

Chapter 1
One Thing I Can Do

I'm Josh Linfoot and I'm nothing, see? No one. Know how that feels, do you? I mean, I was here first, before my sister, but that doesn't count. No. What counts is being brainy. Doing well at school.

My sister's brainy. Beth. She does well at school. Mum and Dad love her, they don't give a stuff about me. It's always been like that, since the day she was born. Beth this. Beth that. See what Beth can do.

1

But there's one thing I can do really well. Really well. I can start fires.

I'm in Mitch Mitchell's gang. His brother Danny's in my class. He got me into it.

It's Friday, afternoon break. Danny and me are talking. I goes, "Saturday tomorrow. Long, boring day."

Danny's like, "I'm never bored."

"How come?" I says.

Danny grins. "Fires. We start fires. It's wicked."

I stare at him. "Fires," I goes. "What sort of fires?"

"All sorts," he says. "Bins, cars, sheds. Schools, sometimes."

"Schools?" He's having a laugh. Must be.

Danny nods. "Oh, yeah. Remember when Colton High went up, a few years back?"

My turn to nod. "'Course. It was on the news, wasn't it? Million quid damage. Don't tell me you ..."

"Yeah – well, not me, I was only twelve. It was my brother and his mates."

I stare at him. "Your brother did Colton High?"

"Yeah, and they never got him, did they? Never will. He's too smart." He looks at me. "Why don't you come with us? It'll be something to do."

"W-when?"

"Tomorrow, if you like."

"You're doing one tomorrow?" It doesn't sound real.

"We'll be doing *something*."

"What about your brother?" I ask. "Won't he mind me turning up?"

Danny grins. "No, he won't mind. If I say you're a mate of mine. You are a mate of mine, aren't you, Josh?"

I smile, but my heart's booting me in the ribs. "'Course I am, Danny."

"Three o'clock then, bus shelter by the ice rink."

I'm in a daze the rest of the afternoon. And all night. Mitch Mitchell's nineteen. He does what he likes, he's well cool. Flip Dolton's in his gang, and Ram Dass. They're hard, those guys. You don't stare at them. I can't believe they're going to let someone like me tag along.

Turns out they aren't keen at all. When I get there, it's just Danny and Mitch in the shelter. The others are late.

I grin. "Hi, Mitch," I say, dead cool.

He eyeballs me. "Listen, kid," he growls. "You're here because this runt ..." he smacks

4

Danny across the back of the head, hard,
"... this runt blabbed to you about gang stuff."

I look at Danny. He's trying not to cry.
Mitch grabs his hood, jerks him in, starts
smacking him again. "We never (smack)
never (smack) never (smack) blab gang stuff
to anyone, not even to make ourselves feel
big." He shakes his little brother. "Feel big,
do you, runt?"

"N – no Mitch." Danny's crying now.
I don't want to look at him. It's my fault he's
in trouble.

"Look," I croak, "I'll just go, alright?
I didn't mean to cause ..."

Mitch shakes his head. "You're going
nowhere, kid – you know too much. I've got a
little job ready for you, and when you've done
it you'll be one of us. Which means ..." he
grins, "if we go down, you go down."

The others show up just then. Bobby Robinson, Flip Dolton, Ram Dass and Tony Parsons. Mitch tells them my name, says I'll be around from now on. He doesn't tell me their names – no need. Everyone in our town knows who they are. Knows them and fears them. Being in that bus shelter with them feels like being a tadpole in a pond of piranhas.

Chapter 2
Baby Seat

There's a 4-by-4 standing on waste ground where the steelworks used to be. It's a silver Marauder.

"There you go, kid," growls Mitch. "All yours."

I look at him. "Whose is it?" I ask.

"I told you," he murmurs. "Yours. Light it up."

"I ... haven't got a light."

"Oh, for Pete's sake." The others snigger, except Danny. He's still not looking at me. Mitch fishes in his pocket, hands me a lighter. "Go on."

I walk towards the 4-by-4. It's nearly new. No way did the owner park it here. The lads must have nicked it earlier, that's why they were late. I'm shaking, my legs have gone weak. I can feel the gang's eyes on me. This is a test, to find out if I'm good enough to be a member.

I don't want to do it. They can't force me. But they'll beat me up. They might even dump me in the Marauder and set it on fire. I shiver and go up to the driver's door.

It isn't locked. The door swings open. I boost myself inside. One of the back seats is fitted with one of those baby seats. Beside the baby seat is a box of tissues. I grab it, pull out all the tissues and dump them on the baby seat. I tear the box in two and lay it on top. Then I flick the lighter and touch the flame to the tissues.

I'm really, really scared, but it's an amazing feeling, watching that little flame grow. In seconds the back of the baby seat is alight. Plastic foam starts to melt and trickle down. Thick black smoke pours out. I'm kneeling on the driver's seat. I'm looking at what I've done. I'm just watching, watching …

A voice starts yelling. It's Mitch. "Get out, you little plonker!" he roars. "D'you want to go up with it or what?"

I turn and jump out of the car. The fire's only been going for seconds, but the heat is terrific. Unbelievable. I leave it behind and run to where I can watch. I'm coughing from the smoke. My eyes are watering. I knuckle them. All I want is to watch.

Danny was right. It's wicked. The Marauder is a boiling, roaring furnace – like the steelworks all over again. As I watch there's an explosion – crrrump! I feel the blast. A fireball like an H-bomb rolls up through the smoke. *I did this*, I think. *Me, Loser Linfoot. Who's a loser now, eh?*

There's people beginning to notice the fire now. The motorway flyover's not far off. Cars are stopping, drivers like little dolls up there, pointing. Mitch sees them. "Right," he snaps. "Time to split. Hurry it up, kid."

We scatter. We head for the little streets behind the waste ground. A siren wails. When I stop for a breather, it's just me and Danny.

I grin and wipe the sweat off my face with my sleeve. "That was awesome," I gasp. "The way it went up, in seconds."

Danny nods. He leans on a wall. "Now you know why I'm never bored."

"Sure do. What about tomorrow?" I ask.

He laughs. "Nothing tomorrow. Gang's got other stuff to see to. Business. Mitch don't like us kids around then. I'll see you at school Monday."

We split up. I'm dying to go back, watch the firemen tackle the blaze. *My* blaze. But I don't. I go home.

"You smell funny," goes Beth, the second I walk in. Nine years old, eyes like a hawk, nose like a sniffer dog. Nothing gets by Beth.

"Bonfire," I grunt, "up the allotments."

I go to my room, change my kit before Mum smells me too. After tea I watch the local news, but there's nothing about the fire. Shame.

But the story's not over. I wake up sweating and shaking in the middle of the night. I've had a dream about the baby seat. A nightmare. I was watching the flames

catch hold when something moved. I saw
there was a baby in the car seat. It sat
kicking like they do and waving its arms
about. Too young to know what was
happening. It kept reaching for the flames.
I started to run back towards the car. I was
crying out, *I didn't know*. But I was beaten
back by the heat. The baby seat was melting
and tipping to one side. The kid started to
cry now and stretched chubby arms towards
me. I tried, but I couldn't get near. I saw the
baby's soft skin begin to blister and smoke. It
was so horrible, so real, I had to wake up to
escape.

It was a warning, that nightmare, but I
didn't know. Didn't know there are
nightmares you can't escape, 'cos you're not
asleep.

Chapter 3
Dope

I'm excited when I walk into school Monday morning. I'm a new Josh Linfoot today. I'm sure people will know by the way I look. There goes Josh, they'll whisper. Josh the firestarter – one of Mitch Mitchell's gang.

Doesn't happen. Nothing happens, except Danny asks if I'm all right. "Cool," I tell him. I hope he'll say something about next Saturday, but he nods and walks off. Still getting grief from big brother, I expect.

Turns out I won't have to wait till Saturday. Tuesday morning Danny moves up to me and says, "Tonight, half-six, allotment gates."

I corner him at lunchtime. I ask, "What is it tonight?"

"Shed job," he says. "Shed and greenhouse."

"Whose?" My dad's got an allotment. I hope we aren't after his shed.

"Wait and see," he goes. "Gang stuff. Bring a lighter this time."

Sarky sod. I always carry a lighter now, sort of like a badge. To show I'm a member.

****

It's drizzling at half-six. Getting dark. There'll be no gardeners about on this nasty March evening. Mitch opens the gate and we troop along the path. "This is the one," he says.

There's a rickety gate in the hedge. Ram Dass kicks it down and we trample it as we go into the allotment.

It's a good shed. Thick pine boards, newish, stained with creosote paint. It stands on a brick base. There's a window in the side and a little one in the door. The door's padlocked. "Get the lock," says Mitch, and Tony Parsons moves to obey. The rest of us turn to the greenhouse.

It's newish, like the shed. Big, too. "Room for lots of tomatoes to grow in here," I say.

"Tomatoes!" Mitch spits the word. "Heated unit, that. You can grow dope in there. And sell it on. Make a nice bit of dosh. That's what this guy was going to do for me. But he wimped out."

Mitch picks up a stone. "The greenhouse won't burn. We'll do the glass," he said.

We do the glass with stones, boots and a spade from the shed. I get nervous, it makes so much noise. But no one comes. Who'd be daft enough to bother? It's dark and there's seven of us.

I want to light the shed, but Ram gets the job. He's found a can of paraffin. Perfect. We watch him splash it everywhere, inside and out. Then he soaks a rag in it and chucks it into the shed.

The shed goes up with a whoosh. Paraffin's good, but creosote's better. There's a drum that's left from when the shed was stained. When the flames reach it we all cheer. The explosion blows out a side of the shed. Sparks whirl on the damp air. What's left of the shed sags, crackling. Roof felt burns well, too.

Soon we hear sirens. We have to leave the fire, but we don't run off. There are plenty of shadowy places to hide. Danny and I head for the next-door allotment. There's a shed there too. An old one. We slide between that and the hedge. "Get some stones," Danny hisses.

The firemen drive an engine along the pathway, run out the hose, start looking for a tap. Showers of stones come from the darkness, like hail. The firemen dodge about. They're cursing and swearing, putting their arms up to cover their faces. One's on his mobile. "He's calling for back-up," raps Danny. "Get him."

We pelt the guy till he scuttles behind the vehicle, where he comes under attack from another direction. Why am I not scared stiff? I should be. But I'm not. There's no time to be scared. I'm pumped up, high as a kite. I want it to go on forever.

It doesn't. After a few minutes come more sirens, blue flashes, sounds of barking. "Police dogs," cries Danny. "Come on."

We get away. Everyone runs for it. I admit, I was scared when I heard those dogs, but we never saw them. And what a rave! I've smashed glass, watched a blaze, used living guys for target practice. All in all, it's the most excitement I've had in a long time. The most *ever*.

Who needs dope when you're totally hooked on fire?

Chapter 4
Want Locking Up

"What on earth's happened, Josh?" goes Mum when I walk in. "You look as if you've been dragged through a hedge backwards."

I know I'm a mess, got my excuse ready. "We were in the park, Mum. Me and Danny. Some big lads chased us. We ran into the bushes to get away, but it was all mud and dead leaves."

"*I* don't know." Mum shakes her head. "Fourteen, and still playing kids' games. I hope you'll grow out of it one day."

"It wasn't a *game*, Mum," I protest. "The guys chasing us were muggers. They were after our phones. It's not like when you were young."

"Hmm. Well, you better go clean yourself up before your dad gets back." Dad's in a quiz team down the pub Tuesdays. I don't know how he stands the excitement.

There's excitement next day as well. I get in from school and Dad's home already. He's an estate agent, no fixed hours. I know by his red face something's got him stirred up. "Something up, Dad?" I ask.

"I'll say." He's got the local paper. He flaps it in my face. "Look at this." I squint at the front page photo. My heart lurches. It's the allotment we trashed last night. *He knows*, goes a voice inside my skull. *I'm dead.*

He doesn't know, thank God. But then he starts up again. "Look at it," he bellows. "Where's the sense in that? Jim Pickard owned that shed. He spent hundreds of pounds last year, putting in a new greenhouse, new shed. Just so some brainless goons can come along and destroy it all."

"It's – rotten," I mutter. "Those guys want locking up."

"Locking up?" Dad throws the paper across the kitchen. It falls apart all over the quarry tiles. "They'd get more than locking up if I could get my hands on 'em. *Throttling*, that's what they deserve. *Flogging* ..."

"Alan," goes Mum softly. She's picking up the sheets of newspaper. "It's no use getting upset. The men who did this are miles away by now. They won't be caught, so you might as well put it out of your mind. Think about something nice, like Beth's news."

"What's Beth's news?" I ask. I don't want to hear what else Dad would do if he got his hands on me. I don't want to hear about my sister's latest miracle either, but it'll stop Dad going on about that allotment job.

Mum smiles. "I'll let her tell you herself," she says. "She'll be down in a minute."

Soon the four of us're sitting round the table, eating pizza and chips. Beth's still wearing her school cardie – she wants us to see her new badge. It's green to match the cardie, with the word ZOO-KEEPER in gold. I look at her.

"Zoo-keeper?" I say.

She nods. "Yes. Mr Hartley's put us in charge of all the animals. Me and Kate. He had these badges specially made."

"Ah-ha!" I nod. "Mr Hartley. Bit gone on Mr Hartley, aren't you, sis?"

"No, I'm *not*." She's gone red.

"What you blushing for, then?" I ask.

"I'm not blushing."

Mum breaks in. Doesn't like me having a go at my sister. "Tell Josh what Mr Hartley said to you and Kate, sweetheart," Mum says.

"Oh ..." Beth looks down at her plate. She's chuffed to bits, but she's good at acting modest. "He said he was giving us a responsible job because we've proved to be mature, responsible people. He said he's known plenty of adults who weren't nearly as sensible as me and Kate. He said the animals are in the safest possible hands." She glances up, embarrassed. "That's all."

"*All?*" I snort. "Wish someone'd say something like that about *me*, even if it was only once."

As I say this, something swells in my throat. A big sore lump. I jump up and run out of the room.

23

I lie on my bed and cry, because what I said to my sister is true. Josh Linfoot, firebug in Mitch Mitchell's gang, would swop his lighter for his sister's badge in a flash, if only it were that easy.

If only.

Chapter 5
Cut Price Day

"I see we made the front page, Josh." It's Thursday morning, just before the bell goes. Danny sounds dead chuffed.

"What? Oh, yeah." I'm not chuffed. I had the baby seat nighmare again, hardly slept after.

"Mitch is well pleased," says Danny. "That Pickard guy tried to make a prat out of him, and no one makes a prat out of our Mitch."

I look at him. "Does he know who did it? Bit obvious. He knows Mitch has a grudge against him. What if he tells the police?"

Danny shakes his head. "Not a chance. Mitch knows where he lives, him and his family. If you can burn a shed you can burn a house. Pickard knows that."

"You mean ...?" I gulp. "Mitch'd set fire to a house with people inside?"

Danny shrugs. "I dunno. Don't think so ... But Pickard won't want to take the chance." He grins. "Quit worrying, Josh. Mitch knows what he's doing."

Danny doesn't say anything about Saturday. I sort of hope we won't be doing anything, but a part of me – the part that's hooked on fire – can't help but hope we might.

Dawdling home Friday afternoon, Danny says, "Cut-price day down Tesco's tomorrow, Josh."

I frown. "So?"

"So we're the guys to make it happen. You and me."

I shake my head. "I don't know what you're on about, Danny. Make what happen?"

He puts an arm round me and tells me. He keeps his voice low.

****

Midday Saturday, the seven of us are at Tesco's. We all got there different ways and at different times. We grab trolleys, start shopping. It's as if we don't know one another.

I cruise the DIY, hardware and motorist aisles. I load my trolley with paint, white spirit, motor oil and rubber mats. I get candles too, and firelighters and ten boxes of matches in a carton. I'm not loading this stuff at random – it's all part of Mitch's cunning plan. I don't look but I know Danny's choosing the same stuff as me. He's stacking it in his trolley and undoing a screwcap here and there without letting anyone see.

I look at my watch. 12.27. Three minutes to zero. I swing my trolley round and wheel it towards the back left-hand corner of the store, near the hanging plastic strips over the doorway to the warehouse. I take my time. Mitch says it's always best not to hurry. People in a hurry get noticed.

12.29. I take the lighter out of my pocket. Take a quick look round.

No one watching. I click, get a tiny flame. One last timecheck. 12.30 on the dot. I bend over the trolley, touch the flame to the corner of a rubber mat. It catches at once, because some white spirit has dribbled onto it from a leaky cap. You've got to be really careful with flammable stuff. I roll the trolley right in under the hanging strips and walk away. I take my time. In the back right-hand corner, Danny's doing the same.

I'm outside when the alarm begins to wail. I turn and stand and watch, just like anyone else. Inside the store, they're telling customers to file out in an orderly manner, leaving trolleys and heavy bags behind. People are leaving, all right, but it isn't orderly. There's a lot of pushing and shoving, most of all near the door. There are trolleys too, and bags. Customers are close to panic, if you ask me, and you can't blame them. It's a big place, but the store is quickly filling with thick black smoke – the sort you get from paint and rubber. Tesco's people are running about like headless chickens. They're trying to do what they should when there's a fire – to follow the fire drill. But the customers just take no notice.

And so no one sees that five of the trolleys crowding the two exits are piled high with state-of-the-art electronic stuff. The security guys should be watching the doors. But they've gone pelting up to the back of the store. There are two trolleys ablaze back there, and some plastic strips that are carrying flames to the ceiling. And no one will notice when those five trolleys at the front go missing. There's too much going on everywhere else.

I'd love to stay and watch, but it isn't in the plan. You can't throw stones at firemen in a great open car park. And anyway, ten thousand quid's-worth of electronics is enough fun for one day.

One cut-price day.

Chapter 6
Getting Out Of Hand

Mitch promises me and Danny fifty quid each for our blaze-in-a-basket stunt. "You'll have to wait," he warns us. "Cops'll be on the look-out for the stuff we nick. We'll sit on it for a bit, then sell it when the fuss dies down."

Turns out the wait is the least of our worries. Most of all for me. Saturday, a Tesco's customer saw a boy with a trolley who was acting odd. She's got a good memory. The police get her to do a photo-fit.

Wednesday, I pick the paper off the mat when I get in from school and there's her photo-fit. It's in the middle of the front page. It looks so like me I could use it in my passport.

I nearly mess my pants. I might as well turn round right now, march down to the police station, show them the photo-fit and give myself up. In fact that might be safer than waiting for Dad to get home.

I could hide the paper. Chuck it in the bin or pretend it's not come today. Or I could pack a bag and run off.

I don't do any of those things. I decide the only thing to do is tough it out. I put the paper on the table, change out of my uniform and help Mum get the meal. Act as if nothing's wrong. If someone picks up the paper, and gasps, and blurts out that the photo-fit looks just like me, then I'll get all cross. I'll say they must be blind – it's nothing like me.

Well – what else can I do?

The next few hours are unreal. I peel the spuds, put them on to boil. When she's setting the table, Beth picks up the paper. I watch her as she scans the front page. I wait for her to yell, "Hey, Mum – there's a picture of Josh in the paper." It doesn't happen. She puts the paper down and goes on setting the table. I can't believe it.

Not long after that I hear the car on the drive. Dad's home. By this time I'm really tensed up. I can't just wait till he picks up the paper. As he opens the kitchen door, I run upstairs. I shut myself in my room. I'll stay here till I hear him start shouting, then go down and confess. To be perfectly honest, it'll be good to get it over.

Five minutes pass. Then ten. Dad *must* have looked at the paper by now – it's the first thing he does on a Wednesday teatime. A habit. Maybe he's waiting, ready to grab me when I come down. Perhaps he's already on the phone to the police.

"Josh." Mum calls up the stairs. "Meal's ready, we're waiting for you."

I bet you are, I think. But her voice sounds normal – no strain or anything. I hope mine sounds normal too as I reply, "OK, Mum – just coming."

They're sitting round the table. Dad gives me one of his looks as I sit down. Mum says, "What were you doing up there, Josh – homework?"

"Yeah," I mumble. "Geography." Well, I can't tell the truth, can I? The paper lies folded by Dad's plate. Hasn't he looked at it yet?

He *has* looked at it. As Mum's getting the pudding, he flicks the paper with his knuckles. "Getting out of hand, all this," he growls.

"What's that, Dad?" I ask

"This." He picks up the paper, opens it, shows me the front page. I swallow hard, gazing at the photo-fit that looks just like me. "Oh, the Tesco thing."

Dad nods grimly. "Yes, the Tesco thing, as you call it. Setting fire to the place, just so they could pinch some electronics. Hundreds of people inside. Miracle no one was killed."

I nod and push my food round the plate. "Yes, it is." *What about the picture?* I think. *Can't you see it's your loser son, Dad?* But I don't say this out loud, of course.

"I bet it's the same lot who torched Jim Pickard's allotment," Dad goes on.

I don't reply straight away – can't trust my voice. After a bit I say, "Could be, I suppose – but it's not the same sort of thing really, is it?"

Dad starts shouting then. "It's *exactly* the same, Joshua. Total lack of respect for other people's property. Not to mention putting lives at risk. Scum like that should be kept right away from normal people. Put them all on an island somewhere. Let 'em set each other on fire if they want to – just keep 'em away from everyone else."

All the time he's yelling this, he's waving the newspaper about. And there's my picture in it. I can't believe no one's noticed how the photo-fit looks just like me. Not my mum, not my dad or my sister. I think it's because they never really look at me. Of course a neighbour might see that it's me, or a teacher at school. I seem to have got away with it at home. But I'm not kidding myself I'm off the hook.

****

It's the weekend before I even start to relax. Every minute I'm expecting someone's hand to land on my back and tell me I'm nicked. All day Thursday and Friday I wait for the police to walk in the classroom with the Head. They'll call me out and shove me in a car. I expect Danny to say something about the photo-fit, but he doesn't. I can't believe it when Friday afternoon crawls round at last and I'm still free.

I know why I'm feeling like this. It's my conscience. I know I'm doing bad stuff, and my conscience is what made me see myself in the photo-fit. I expect the photo-fit isn't much like me at all. Can't be, can it, or somebody would finger me.

I wish now I'd listened to my conscience. I wish it every time I look at my sister.

Chapter 7
Tinfoil Barbs

We don't do anything that weekend. I'm glad. It's no fun being tense all the time. Saturday I go with Mum, Dad and my sister to the garden centre. Yes, I *know*. Sad, but I need to relax. Dad's buying stuff for the allotment – seeds and that. Me and Beth go to the aquarium section. Water features, tanks, tropical fish. We stand watching the tinfoil barbs. They're my favourite. It's dead restful, watching them.

"Mr Hartley got tinfoils?" I ask my sister.

She shakes her head. "Goldfish," she says. "And an axolotl."

"What the heck's an axolotl?"

Beth grins. "It's like a giant tadpole. If you feed it too much it turns into a lizard thing – a salamander."

"So how often do you feed it?"

"Once a month," she says.

"And what does it get to eat, then, every month?"

"A big worm."

"Ugh!" I pull a face. "Glad I'm not an axolotl then. What about the goldfish?"

"They get fed every day. Well – every *school* day. They can manage over the weekend, as long as you give them plenty of food on Fridays." She smiles. "Same goes for

the hamsters and gerbils and guinea pigs. Me
and Kate fix extra water bottles to the cages
on Friday afternoons, so they'll have enough
till Monday."

I nearly puke, listening to her showing off.
But I need to listen. I'm starting to get a
brilliant idea.

Mum calls us away then, and we drive
home. Dad's in a bad mood. He'd bumped into
his pal, Jim Pickard, in the garden centre. Jim
was buying a new shed to replace the one
we'd torched. "Three hundred and forty quid,
it's costing him," growls Dad. "Pity he can't
get the idiots who burned his other one to
pay."

Dad seems to be watching me in the car
mirror, so I nod. "Yeah. Make 'em think
twice, that would," I say. How cool do I
sound? Tinfoil barbs should be on the
National Health, for stress. Who'd know what
I'm feeling inside.

Nothing happens on Sunday. I don't go with Dad to the allotment. I bet he and his mate are hammering nails into Jim's three hundred and forty quid shed. They'll be saying stuff like, "I wish we were hammering these into those bad guys." Just what I need.

Not.

Fire, that's what I need. A good fire. Not one that'll get me arrested. A lawful fire. And I'm lucky. Last autumn, Dad tidied our back garden. Cut back the shrubs and that. He does it every November. He calls it putting the garden to bed for the winter. He piles up the rubbish at the bottom of the garden, lets it dry out a bit, then sets fire to it. And he lets me help. It's the only bit of gardening I enjoy.

Last autumn it didn't dry out. Or maybe the neighbours always had washing out or something. Anyway, we didn't burn the rubbish, so it lay there all winter. It's there now.

"Mum?" I say. "Is it OK if I burn the garden rubbish?"

"I suppose," she says. "As long as you're careful and don't let it scorch the fence. Fire spreads, you know."

Tell me about it, I think but don't say.

It's not a bad fire. Not as good as Jim Pickard's shed, of course, but not bad. I beg a firelighter off Mum, shove it right in at the bottom. Dad reckons it's cheating, using firelighters. Real gardeners use old newspapers and a few dry sticks. A firelighter's less hassle. One touch of the old lighter and it's away. Nothing puts it out.

Most of the stuff's pretty damp, and there's a lot of thick smoke at first. Plenty of spitting and crackling as well.

The flames are just getting a good hold when I see something move at the foot of the heap. A toad. It must have spent the winter asleep under the rubbish. It comes crawling out, moving pretty smartly for a toad. It's not hurt, just surprised and a bit scared. I watch it head for a stand of daffodil shoots, then I don't see it any more.

As I look into the heart of the blaze, I soon forget the toad. Watching a fire you've started drives everything else out of your mind. It's beautiful and powerful. Nothing can resist it, and it's there because of you. You're its creator, it does what you want it to do.

Like I say, I forget the toad. But I think it gets saved on my hard drive, because that night it downloads while I'm asleep and I have another horrible dream.

I'm watching the fire. The toad crawls out, only this time it's left it too late. Its back end is smoking. The warty skin has begun to melt and trickle down. But the worst thing is, the poor thing's screaming.

Toads don't scream. I know that, even in my dream, but this one's screaming, and it's all my fault. I pick up the smoking toad and look for some water to drop it in. There's a bucket of water just by me, but when I drop it in, the toad comes in two. The front half falls into the bucket, the back half stays stuck to my hand. Now *I'm* screaming. I shake and shake my hand again and again. I feel totally sick, but the toad clings to me till I wake up.

I have to switch on my bedside light and look at my hand in the glow before I know for sure it was just a dream. And even then it's ages before I get back to sleep.

Chapter 8
Jack Potty

Two weeks pass. Nothing happens. It says in the paper the police are still investigating the Tesco incident, but they never question Mitch. Never come near any of us. Each day I feel more relaxed. Then it's the start of the Easter holidays.

Monday, Danny calls my moby. I must be psychic, because I'm asking myself right then when I'm going to see the fifty quid Mitch promised. "Normal place," Danny raps. "Seven o'clock tonight. Payday."

"That's amazing," I cry. "I was just thinking about that dosh when – "

Danny cuts in. "Don't burble, Josh. Not on the phone. Never know who might be earwigging. And don't say anything to anyone. See you at seven."

The day drags a bit after that. Well, I've never had fifty quid at one time. Can't wait to feel those crisp notes on my palm. I saw this cowboy film one time on TV. It was about a bounty hunter. That's someone that goes out and brings the baddies in and gets a reward. Doesn't matter if the baddies come back dead or alive. Anyway, the guy in this film has just brought in a body and got his cash. Someone asks him why he's a bounty hunter and he says, "I'm counting the reasons." Then he smiles and counts the dollar bills in his hand. And that cash was just for shooting a guy, which maybe he enjoyed doing anyway. *I'd* smile if I was him.

Like I'll be smiling at seven o'clock when I get *my* cash.

I'm thinking Mitch'll be there to pay us out, but it's just Danny. He checks up and down the road, then pulls a load of notes out of his backpack. Fives. He lays them on my palm and I flick through them like the bounty hunter, counting. There are ten fives. I grin. "Why do we start fires, Danny?" I ask, and before he can answer, I'm like, "I'm counting the reasons."

Danny shakes his head. "You're a nut, Josh Linfoot. I always said so." He nods towards my dosh. "Put it in your pocket, take it straight home, hide it. *Not* in your room."

I look at him. "Why not in my room? Where else am I gonna hide it?"

He gives a sigh. "Your mum knows every hiding place in your room, dummy. Trust me. She's checked them out a hundred times for drugs, ciggies, weapons, dodgy magazines."

47

He smiles. "It's what mums do. Our rooms are private, but only when we're there."

"OK." I nod. "But *where*, then?"

"Your dad has a shed, I've seen it." He looks at me. "Find something in there that hasn't been moved for years. Something in a dark corner, with broken stuff all covered in cobwebs. A plant pot or a rusty tin. Shove it in there, only be careful not to break the cobwebs. Don't disturb the dust."

I smile. I've just thought of something. "There's Beth's potty," I tell him. "The potty she had when she was a baby. I don't know why my mum and dad've kept it, but it's been in the shed for at least four years. It used to be pink, but it's sort of greyish-yellow now, and stuff's fallen on top of it – old jam jars, a bicycle pump, a broken deck-chair. Stuff that'll never be used again."

Danny nods. "Well there you go. Shove it in the potty, call it your jack-potty." He's witty, old Danny. Then he gets serious. "Never have more than one fiver on you. We don't want people asking why we're so rich all of a sudden. That's why Mitch paid us in fives, so we won't flash it around."

I do what Danny says. It makes sense. I keep a fiver back, and put the rest in the potty without disturbing anything. Forty-five quid. It gives me a good feeling, knowing it's there. And I'm really careful with the five I keep back. Anyway I'm not one to show off my cash.

I feel rich, but that's not enough. Now I'm not thinking that I might get arrested any day, I need some other excitement. I start wishing Mitch would choose something for us to burn.

And there's something else. It's about my sister, Beth. I've always had to listen to my folks going on about how wonderful Beth is, but now it seems all they can talk about is this zoo-keeper business. You'd think she'd won the lottery or something. It's Beth this and Beth that. Beth's so sensible. So reliable. So mature. Mature. She's nine years old, for Pete's sake. It's doing my head in.

I did say before that I'd started to get a brilliant idea, yeah? Well, this is when I decide to go ahead with it. Looking back, later on, it sounds insane, but at the time it seems OK to me. Clever, even. Here's how I'm thinking.

I need excitement.

The most exciting thing is fire.

Mitch doesn't seem to be planning a fire any time soon.

I could plan one myself, there's nothing to it.

My sister's zoo-keeper job is doing my head in – it's got to go.

If the school burns, Beth's zoo'll burn too.
I get my fire, and her job goes up in smoke.
End of problem.

Good, eh?

****

I make my plan. I don't write it down or
anything – I'm not daft. It's all in my head.

I'll work alone, I decide. Even Danny won't
know about it. I'll make sure no one sees me
– no photo-fit pictures this time. I'll do it on
a Saturday when the school's empty. Empty
except for those gerbils and guinea-pigs.
That axolotl. I'll go straight home after I've
done it. That won't be easy – watching's the
best bit, but the whole point of my plan is to
make Mum think I've been in my room all the
time.

There's this little roof under my window.
Roof of the kitchen extension. If I hang by my
fingers from my sill, my toes just reach it.

I've left the house that way loads of times when I've wanted to dodge homework or stuff like that. Getting back up's a bit harder. I have to jump up, hook my fingers on the sill and swing sideways to get one foot on the overflow pipe. But I *can* do it. The best bit is, we've got a huge tree in the back garden. No nosy neighbours'll see anything.

How hard can it be to commit the perfect crime?

I know what you're thinking: *what about those poor animals*, right? Well, what about me? I've been Josh the loser ever since I can remember. Josh the spare part. Josh the waste of space. I've been shoved aside and dumped on, so don't expect me to care about a few rodents and a flipping axolotl, 'cos I don't. Why should I?

Chapter 9

The Secret Of Good Planning

I don't do it in the holidays. I want to get that zoo, and it's not there in school holidays. Kids take the animals home. One of the guinea-pigs arrived in Beth's room the day we broke up. It'll be there till we go back.

Why wait to destroy the zoo? Why don't I settle for just torching the school? Now, later, I really, really wish I had, but it's no use wishing, is it?

So, Easter rolls by and the summer term begins. Beth lugs the guinea-pig back to school. Kate brings back the axolotl. The zoo's open for business.

I work on my plan. The big day's going to be the second Saturday of term. On the first Saturday, I spend some time watching the place. I see how old Fallon, the caretaker, potters around, doing stuff in the yard. When he needs to go inside the building, he uses the kitchen door round the back. The main entrance stays locked.

This is a bit of a shame. I was hoping Fallon went in and out the front way. Then I'd be sure he was out of the school before I lobbed my petrol bomb. That's how I'm planning to start the fire. I'm going to fill a bottle full of petrol, cork it with a rag, then set light to the rag and chuck the whole lot into the school.

But I'm not a psycho. I don't want to kill Fallon. I want to be sure he's in his house at the front of the school when I chuck the bomb in. If he's at the front, it's easy. Out comes Fallon, into his house and then – in goes the bomb! Then I'm off.

If I chuck the thing in at a side window, it'd make a big noise and Fallon'll come running. I might not have time to vanish.

I change my plan. I can't throw the bomb through the kitchen door, because Fallon locks it every time he leaves. It'll have to go in through a window right at the back. Fallon won't hear that, plus it'll be easy for me to escape the back way. I'll watch Fallon cross to his house, then slip round and do the job.

Think of everything – that's the secret of good planning.

Dad's untidy shed comes in handy again. When I hid my dosh, I saw an old red can on a shelf. It's the sort of can drivers sometimes carry, with spare petrol, in case they run dry in the middle of nowhere. This one's empty, but that's good. I'll take it to the petrol station to fill up. If you're going to show up on foot at a filling-station, wanting a few litres of petrol, it's a good idea to have the right sort of container. If you turn up with a pop bottle or something made of plastic, people get suspicious. Most of all if you're young. They're like, *what does he want petrol for? What's he going to do with it?* With the official red can, no one's bothered. You learn all this stuff if you hang out with guys like Mitch.

I go on Sunday evening. It's dusk. Dad's down the pub, Mum and Beth gawping at the telly. I take a fiver from the old potty. At the filling station, I stick the nozzle in the can and get three litres. The guy takes my money, gives change, says g'night.

Easy.

I put the can back on the shelf, in exactly the same spot. Well, it's stood there years, nobody's touched it. Why should they touch it now?

The week drags a bit. I need excitement, and all I get is the same old stuff about Beth the magic zoo-keeper. *Not for much longer*, I keep telling myself, but it feels like forever.

I keep myself from telling Danny. It's not easy, but I've decided to work alone. Part of my plan. I might tell him after, to boost my cred with the gang. Might. It'll depend how it goes.

Friday night I say to Mum, "Think I better start revising tomorrow, unless you want me for something."

I've just come in from filling a pop bottle with petrol from the red can. I've hidden the bottle up the side of the shed. Mum doesn't know this, of course. She doesn't want me for anything. I knew she wouldn't. She's always on at me to revise, she can't believe her luck. She's like, "No, you're all right, son. Stay in your room, I'll knock with a cuppa now and then."

I shake my head. "No cuppas, Mum, thanks. I'll take a few Cokes up. Only keep Beth out of my hair, eh?"

Sheer genius. No one's going to open my door. No one'll know I'll be missing for an hour or so. It's perfect.

****

Saturday dawns wet and windy. I don't care. In fact it's good. No nosy neighbours in gardens. Easier for me to get out and back. I eat breakfast with Mum. My sister's having a lie-in, Dad's gone to the office. As soon as I've finished I go up to my room and close the door. Rain rattles on the window, the tree outside sways and ripples in the wind. I switch on my computer, watch it boot up.

It's half-eight. I'll give it an hour, then go. I pretend to revise, but I can't concentrate. Don't try. I'm just passing the time. Beth's moby chirps. I hear her get up and scamper downstairs. She whines and moans on about something, I can't hear what. Don't *want* to hear. She's always moaning about something.

At half-nine I get into my hoodie, open the window and climb out. It's still raining, there's no one about. I collect the bottle. I keep an eye on the window in case Mum looks out. She doesn't. I slip away. The bomb's hidden inside my jacket. In a pocket I have my lighter and a spare, plus a bit of rag to stuff down the bottle's neck.

You have to think of everything.

Chapter 10
The Perfect Crime

Twenty to ten. I hide behind a wet bush and watch the school. The front doors are locked. No surprise there. *Where's old Fallon?* I mutter to myself. A second later he walks round the side, dangling his keys. He's been round the back. No surprise there, either. You don't want surprises, that's why you plan.

I watch him cross to his house, go inside, close the door. Perfect. I'll be finished quicker than I thought. I break cover, slant across the yard, walk down the side of the building. No rush, he'll be a few minutes at least.

Halfway down I stop, stand the bottle on a window sill, stuff the rag into the neck. The classroom beyond the window isn't Hartley's. Shame. I'd have liked a glimpse of the zoo before it's too late. But still.

I peep round the corner. No one there, which I knew there wouldn't be. I walk along to the kitchen door, try it. Locked, of course. Hot on security, old Fallon. I click my lighter and set the rag alight. I quiver with excitement as I watch the tiny flame. *Won't be small for long*, I murmur. *Powerful, thanks to me. Destructive. Unstoppable.*

I stand back, pick a window and hurl the bomb.

The effect is stunning. The force of my throw shatters window and bottle together. Petrol, flame and oxygen meet in the air with a sound like nothing I've ever heard. Liquid fire drenches the kitchen. The whole place explodes in a sea of leaping flame.

It's me! I tell myself. I *unleashed this power. I'm the boss of it, it's mine.* I laugh out loud, gazing at my awesome work. For a few seconds I'm totally happy. It's like I'm drunk. For those few seconds I even forget to run. When I *do* leave, I leave laughing.

In a few minutes I'm in my room. A room I've never left. It's the perfect crime.

****

"Josh?" Mum raps on my door. I've only just got out of my hoodie.

"What's up, Mum?"

"Look out of your window. There's smoke. It's near the school. I hope ..."

I've been watching the smoke. Enjoying it. I open the door, forcing myself not to grin. "Hope *what*, Mum?"

She hurries to my window. "I hope it isn't the school. Beth's there."

"*Beth?*" Fear stabs me in the gut. "But it's *Saturday*, Mum. Why would she be at school on a ...?"

"Kate rang. They forgot to leave the animals enough water yesterday. They're there now. It – it does *seem* to be coming from the school."

****

I don't want to talk about it. Oh, they got her out. Her and her little friend. But Beth's ear was burned. Her left ear. You might think she got off light, but not if you saw the way she keeps that side of her face turned away in company. Not if you had to watch how she tries to pull her hair over it all the time. I don't think she knows she's doing it.

They never found out who torched the school, killed the animals, marked Beth for life. Yes, I know – I should've turned myself in and confessed. Easy to say but terribly hard to do. You may think *I* got off light as well, but you're wrong. I have to watch Beth trying to hide her ear. It happens a hundred times a day, and my heart breaks every time, because I love my sister. I never knew I did till Mum said *Beth's there*.

Everyone loves someone. Even a firebug.

Barrington Stoke would like to thank all its readers for commenting on the manuscript before publication and in particular:

Heather Aird
Sam Anderson
Struan Barker
Christopher Bell
Leah Boyle
Courtney Brown
Mark Christie
Michael Corrigon
Connor Gentleman
Keri-Marie Gibson
Connor Hanlon
Daryl Hossack
Nicky Keogh
Morven MacCallum

Natalie MacLaren
Craig MacLean
Alison Massie
John McLoughlin
Sean McTaggart
Andrew Murphy
Tiffany Murray
Sue Phillips
Jacqueline Pollock
Gregor Riggs
Nicola Strathearn
Ross Stevenson
Fiona Watson
Greg Williamson

Become a Consultant!

Would you like to give us feedback on our titles before they are published? Contact us at the email address below – we'd love to hear from you!

info@barringtonstoke.co.uk
www.barringtonstoke.co.uk